For Amanda, Sam, Toby,
and the Oxford Street gang
T. B.

Text copyright © 2009 by Tom Brenner
Illustrations copyright © 2009 by Holly Meade

First edition 2009

Library of Congress Cataloging-in-Publication Data is available.

Library of Congress Catalog Card Number 2008936196

ISBN 978-0-7636-3659-3

2 4 6 8 10 9 7 5 3 1

Printed in China

This book was typeset in Myriad Tilt.
The illustrations were done in watercolor and collage.

Candlewick Press
99 Dover Street
Somerville, Massachusetts 02144

visit us at www.candlewick.com

And Then Comes
HALLOWEEN

TOM BRENNER

illustrated by HOLLY MEADE

CANDLEWICK PRESS

WHEN nighttime creeps closer to suppertime,
and red and gold seep into green leaves,
and blackberries shrivel on the vine . . .

THEN hang dried corn,
still in husks all crinkly and raspy,
sounding like grasshoppers.

WHEN Papa stacks firewood under the eaves,
and a *V* of geese squawks its way south,
and chilly morning air turns noses pink...

THEN cut out paper witches on brooms and dangle skeletons in doorways.

WHEN neighbors rake fallen leaves into piles,
and the sky is that certain deep blue,
and bins of pumpkins arrive at the grocery store . . .

THEN bring one home and scoop and carve,
and, with lights out and candle in,
watch it grin or grimace or wink.

WHEN autumn spiders weave silver webs from pillar to post, and the wind whispers winter, and the bones of trees begin to show . . .

THEN it's time to decide what to be.

WHEN tombstones sprout on lawns like
mushrooms, and ghosts swoop from trees,
and scarecrows stuffed with leaves wave hello ...

THEN the cutting, the sewing, the pasting, the taping, the gluing, and the painting must start.

WHEN the last day of October finally arrives,
and dusk settles itself around hedges and
slips into the grass, and the ticks
and the tocks of the clock take forever . . .

THEN grab your bag or bucket
and sit and stand and pace and
peep out the window
and sit again and stand again.

WHEN Ballerina twirls up
and Buckaroo trots up
and Dragon slithers up
to your door ...

THEN run with friends out into the night,
where the air rings with laughter and shrieks.

Swirl from porch to porch
and knock on doors
to give the password:
"Trick or treat!"

Dart past bushes casting spooky shadows,
sweep past clumps of moaning monsters,
and lug your bursting bag to the next house,
and the next.

WHEN you have plundered your block,
and Ballerina's tutu sags,
and Dragon's tail drags on the ground,
and even the pumpkins look weary . . .

THEN it's time to
go home.

Dump the bags of candy on the floor,

and eat some and count,
and eat some and trade,
and eat some and share
before Dragon and Ballerina
and Buckaroo go home.

AND WHEN your face is washed, and
candy is brushed from your teeth,
and good-night kisses have been given . . .

THEN slip into bed,
draw the quilt to your chin,
and whisper to the darkness,

"Next year...
goggles...
a scarf...
and wings."